TIMMY TIES UP

By Jeremy Moray

Illustrated by Dee Gale

D1441601

Harbour Publishing

AUTHOR'S NOTE

Many thanks to Gary Kleaman for all the help he has given me during the production of the four **Timmy** books; also to Russ Cooper of Westminster Tugs for their photos and historical notes on **BUSTER B**.

J.M.

HARBOUR PUBLISHING
P.O. Box 219
Madeira Park, BC Canada V0N 2H0
Website: www.harbourpublishing.com

Printed and bound in Hong Kong through Colorcraft Ltd.

Canadian Cataloguing in Publication Data

Moray, Jeremy, 1943–
   Timmy ties up

   ISBN 1-55017-055-4

   I. Gale, Dee.   II. Title.
PS8576.0626T5 1991   jC813'.54   C91-091557-1
PZ7.M67Ti 1991

Second printing, 1995
Third printing, 2001
Fourth printing, 2002

for
Emma and Jenny
and their cat
Spencer

ANOTHER AUTHOR'S NOTE

Don't forget to follow the story on the chart at the
back of this book

J.M.

It was a beautiful early summer morning, and Timmy the Tug rocked quietly at the dock on Granville Island. As there was plenty of time for the trip ahead of them, Captain Jones and Frank, the first mate, had decided to go ashore with Matilda, the tug's cat, and have breakfast at the market. John and Derek, the deckhands, went with them to buy the provisions for the journey.

"Where are we going this time?" asked Matilda between laps of milk.

"This is a very special trip," said Captain Jones, "and you mustn't talk about it too loudly, with all these people around us."

He leaned forward and continued in a loud whisper, "We're going to bring a load of dynamite from James Island up to Howe Sound, where it will be loaded onto a ship at night to go to Alaska."

"Dynamite!" meowed Matilda in surprise, and very nearly swallowed her tongue. "Dynamite! But we could blow up!"

"Shshsh," hissed Captain Jones, his finger to his lips, as everybody turned to look at them. "It's quite safe, but not many people know that it goes on, and Howe Sound is the one place where we can load ships at night. Now, finish your milk quickly, and let's get back to Timmy."

As Matilda licked the last drops of milk from her plate, there was a flurry of feathers and Simon the Seagull landed on the chairback beside them, just as Derek and John came out of the Market building loaded down with big brown bags. "Good morning all," said Simon.

Matilda burst out, "Do you know what we are towing as cargo today?" But before she could get any further, Frank swept her up under one arm and they all went off towards Timmy.

Once everything had been stowed away, Captain Jones started up Timmy's engine and they were soon steaming out into English Bay.

They chatted excitedly about the trip ahead of them. "Oh yes," said Timmy, "we used to do this dynamite run quite often. It's always exciting waiting for the ship in the dark off Horseshoe Bay, and then loading the dynamite—quite scary, though."

Matilda gave a little shudder of excitement and snuggled down further into a coil of rope. She was just about to fall asleep when Derek came running up the deck, pointing ahead of them.

"What's on that log out there?" he called. "It looks like a cat."

Captain Jones stuck his head out of the wheelhouse window and peered through his binoculars. "You're right; it IS a cat, clinging to a piece of driftwood," he said.

Matilda jumped up onto the rail to get a better look, and Simon flew off with a loud squawk. "I'll go and see if he's alright," he cried.

"We'd better rescue it," said Captain Jones, and he slowed Timmy down to his slowest speed so that he wouldn't make any waves and tip the cat off the log.

"Well, after all this time, finally we're going to have some company for Matilda," Timmy smiled.

Derek had tied a rope onto a life ring and had it ready to throw to the cat as they came very slowly alongside the log.

"Let me do it," meowed Matilda in her excitement. "After all, it is a cat." Derek gave her the ring. Meanwhile, Frank, guessing what would happen, had gone back to the cabin and found his large landing net. He stood on the stern deck, waiting.

As Timmy came alongside the log, Derek told Matilda to toss the ring over the side into the water. Matilda threw the ring much too hard, and knocked the poor cat off the log.

"Help! Help!" cried the cat, spluttering and clawing at the water. "I can't swim! Help me! Help me!"

Captain Jones saw what was happening and eased Timmy's throttle forward. Frank was ready with the net, and as the cat came past him he lifted it out of the water and put it very gently down on the deck. After much coughing and spluttering, and a good shake, the cat said, "Thank you very much for saving me."

Frank knelt down and picked it up. "What's your name?" he asked.

"Spencer," replied the cat, "and I was running away from home. I don't like my home, so I tried to float out to a ship. I thought I could become a ship's cat. Please don't send me back.

"I had an awful trip on that log; it was so crowded with birds and other animals. . . . . ."

"Don't worry, Spencer; we won't send you home. That is, if you don't mind being a TUG's cat, instead of a SHIP's cat," said Captain Jones.

Just then Simon landed on the rail with a little bundle in his beak wrapped up in a blue and white spotted handkerchief. "Is this yours?" he asked.

"Oh, yes, thank you," replied Spencer. "Those are all my belongings."

"They were still on the log. Matilda didn't manage to knock them off," said Simon, sneering at Matilda, who was gazing with interest at the soggy newcomer.

"Well, you'd better meet your tugmate," said Frank, putting Spencer down on the deck. "This is Matilda, the tug's first cat!"

By early afternoon they were through Active Pass, and making their way down through the islands. Captain Jones talked about how he would like to retire to one of the quiet little bays and live on Timmy. "You could be in command of your own tug," he smiled at Frank, "and take John and Derek with you. Timmy and I could relax here for the rest of our days."

Timmy smiled when he heard this. He thought it was a great idea; after all, he had been working now for nearly seventy years. "So this might be one of my last trips," he thought as they pulled up to the dock on James island where the green and white barge was waiting for them, loaded with dynamite.

The next day as they were approaching Howe Sound, Captain Jones told Derek to winch the barge up closer. As Derek went back to the winch, he heard a lot of squawking and shouting and was nearly tripped up by Spencer and Matilda racing round the corner of the galley, as Simon took off over the side like a rocket.

"What's happening?" cried Derek. Just then he saw clouds of black smoke billowing up around the winch and out of the engine room door beside him. As he turned to run back to the wheelhouse, Timmy's engine spluttered and roared and made terrible banging noises, and finally stopped.

Captain Jones grabbed a fire extinguisher and ran aft with Frank to see what was going on, then he rushed back to the wheelhouse and got on the radio to call the Coast Guard. The two cats dived under the blankets on John's bunk and lay there shivering with fright. Simon flew forward and told Timmy not to worry; he would go and get help from Olly the Octopus and his fire brigade in Horseshoe Bay.

As Simon flew away, Timmy called, "Quick, quick, Simon."

"Flaming flounders," he thought, "what are we going to do? And with all that dynamite just behind me!"

Frank came out of the engine room. But before reporting to Captain Jones in the wheelhouse, he wanted to reassure Timmy.

"It'll be alright, Timmy," said Frank. "Captain Jones has called the Coast Guard, and Derek and John are starting to put the fire out. There's another tug in Centre Bay, and he's coming to take the barge away from us."

"What happened, Frank?" asked Timmy trying not to let big tears roll down his cheeks.

"You've broken a fuel line, and we've got quite a fire in the engine room, but we'll soon have it out. That's what happens to you old tugs." Frank smiled and gave Timmy's brass bell a pat.

Timmy looked up as Simon landed on his rail.

"Olly's on his way, and he's bringing the whole fire brigade with him. And I can see the tug from Centre Bay, he'll be here very soon," said Simon.

It wasn't long before the Coast Guard cutter had a line onto Timmy to hold him steady, while Olly and his firefighters threw buckets of water all over him to stop the fire from spreading through his wooden hull.

At last the danger was over. Derek, Frank and John had managed to put out the fire below and were going into the galley for a rest and a mug of tea. Spencer and Matilda thought they would creep out and see what was happening. They padded gingerly down the deck and peered through the galley door.

"Aha! and where have you been hiding all this time?" asked Frank.

"Oh, we didn't want to get in the way," said Spencer, "so we stayed in John's cabin."

"You didn't want to get wet, you mean!" John and Derek laughed as they picked up the cats and put them on the seat. Suddenly they heard a loud toot. Looking out of the window, they smiled and waved as they saw the tug from Centre Bay towing the dynamite barge away.

By late evening, Timmy was under tow by a cousin of his called Marlin II, and they were heading down the Fraser River to Point Grey Shipyards for repairs.

"Well, that's it," said Captain Jones, taking a big puff on his pipe and turning to Frank. "That's it! Timmy and I are going to retire. We won't just get him repaired, we'll have him converted to a comfy home for me—and the animals, of course!"

"Great idea," said Frank. "When you're all fixed up, Timmy, we'll have a big retirement party." So the dynamite barge was Timmy's last tow, after all.

"Terrific," said Simon, who was floating alongside on the wind. "I'll fly around to all our friends and invite them—especially good old Olly. What a job those Octopi did! I thought they would drown you, Timmy; I've never seen so much water being thrown about."

They all laughed together, and, as the sun set over Vancouver Island, they turned into the Fraser River. Captain Jones took his pipe out of his mouth and began to sing the old Tugboater's Song:

Grab Oronsay's lordly line, clamp her to the dock;
Snatch that drifting gravel barge
(Don't you stop to talk!)
Dodge the mincing yachtsman, scuttle down the tide;
Twist that tanker's tail around,
She's going for a ride
Coastal—Dolmage
(towboat life's a beaut!)
And Gulf of Georgia
HOOT TOOT TOOT!

Soon the wheelhouse was filled with noise as they all sang loudly and stamped their feet, and Timmy laughed happily as Frank made him give several loud toots after each chorus.

The next morning, with Timmy safely tied up alongside the river dock, Captain Jones checked how much damage had been done by the fire. "You look almost as if you *had* been blown up by that dynamite, my friend," said Captain Jones as he clambered about, above and below decks. "It's going to take a month or two to fix you up, I reckon."

Timmy really did look rather a wreck, with great dark smudges and smears all over him from the smoke. In many places his paint had bubbled, blistered and peeled away from the heat of the fire.

Timmy felt very sad that day, because he suddenly realized how much he would miss his busy working days at sea.

Most of all he would miss Derek, John and Frank, who had been his cheerful crew for several years now. They had all had such good times together.

"Never mind, Timmy," said Frank, as he gathered up his belongings, "we will come and visit you while you're being fixed."

"That's right," added Derek, "and we'll come back when you are all shipshape, and take you through the islands to your new home. Then don't forget about that big party Simon's going to organize for you."

The crew members tried to be very jolly as they said goodbye to Timmy and Captain Jones. Matilda and Spencer waved madly from the bows, as Simon circled overhead.

"Well now, Timmy," gruffed Captain Jones, "tomorrow we call in the carpenters!"

A few days later, Mr. Ratolini of Ratty Renovations arrived with several rat helpers. Captain Jones brought some drawings from the aft cabin and walked towards Timmy's bows with Mr. Ratolini, pointing out repairs and alterations that were needed as they went. Mr. Ratty took a pencil from behind his ear and made notes in a little notebook.

Soon the rats were crawling all over Timmy, washing him down with big soft cloths and lots of soap and scraping off peeling paint. Mr. Ratolini himself started measuring up for the alterations to the cabins and other rooms. Timmy heard Captain

Jones talking on a phone, calling for a crane to be brought alongside to lift off the big green winch.

Some days later, Matilda and Spencer decided to go for a walk and explore the dockyard, and hopefully find some mice to play with. As they went over the side, they noticed Simon shoot off and join a long line of seagulls sitting on the roof of one of the buildings nearby.

Simon called to them, "These friends of mine have planned a surprise for Timmy, so be sure you're back on board this afternoon."

After lunch, Timmy was happy to see Frank, Derek and John coming for a visit with Captain Jones. As they clambered aboard, Frank told Timmy how much cleaner he looked already.

Just as they were all talking about the new plans, Matilda and Spencer came over the side paw-in-paw, looking very pleased with themselves. Matilda was about to talk to Captain Jones, when there was a *whooooosh* overhead, and a diamond formation of seagulls swooped over Timmy, with feathers flapping, led by Simon who was flying alongside with a big grin on his face.

Everyone looked up and gasped as the seagull formation headed upwards in a steep climb, and before anyone could say a word, down they came again and flew low over Timmy doing loops and rolls, in a spectacular display of aerobatics, before landing one after the other on Timmy's rail. They were all puffing and panting and looking very smug.

Even Matilda had to whisper to Spencer how incredible she thought they were—she said this very quietly, and when there was plenty of noise from Captain Jones and Frank clapping loudly and the rats shouting "Bravo! Bravo!"

"Thank you, seagulls; that was a terrific air show," called Timmy.

While all this noise was going on, Matilda rubbed up against Timmy's wheelhouse and purred, "Timmy, as my oldest friend, I want you to be the first to know—Spencer wants to marry me!"

"Oh Wow! Oh Whooppee! That means we can have two parties—one for your wedding and one for my retirement! But you will stay with us once you're married, won't you?"

"Of course we will. This is going to be the best home that has ever been built," said Spencer. In his excitement he jumped up and rang Timmy's bell. "There's going to be a wedding," he yowled.

At last the day came when Timmy was all finished. Frank, Derek and John arrived to help Captain Jones take Timmy to his new home in the Gulf Islands.

This was also to be Matilda and Spencer's wedding day.

As Timmy chugged out of the Fraser River, with his new paint sparkling in the morning sun, Captain Jones handed the wheel to Derek and stepped onto the foredeck. Simon and his friends appeared with bunches of wildflowers, just as Captain Jones was getting ready to marry Matilda and Spencer. Matilda was wearing a beautiful veil made from fish net and Spencer had bought a new red bandana for the occasion.

"As Captain, I may perform weddings only in international waters; but we'll make an exception for you cats," said Captain Jones with a chuckle. Just as he was completing the ceremony, there was an enormous splash alongside, as Wally the Whale threw himself in the air and crashed down into the water with a big grin. "Happy wedding! May your shackles never snap!" he called as he disappeared beneath the waves.

After the ceremony, they toasted Matilda and Spencer with glasses of clam juice cocktail, followed by a big seafood feast.

Late in the afternoon, Timmy steamed through Porlier Pass and headed to a small bay on one of the islands. Simon flew off, saying that he was going to deliver invitations to all their friends inviting them to Timmy's retirement party.

The morning of the party, everyone was busy getting Timmy ready, and by early afternoon the guests started arriving. There were the Otters, the Whales, the Octopi and, of course, squadrons of Seagulls. Rackety Raccoon brought his local band, and deer from the island woods came to watch, along with seals, squirrels and an old owl who perched on Timmy's funnel; even some children from a boat anchored nearby came and joined in the dancing.

Captain Jones had invited some people who were living on the island. One of them was a retired sea captain from the B.C. Ferries, so they had a lot to talk about.

Spencer, who loved parties, had been getting rather over-excited and was hanging by his back legs from the wheelhouse roof and making upside-down faces at Timmy. It wasn't long before he fell and did a somersault, landing on the deck on all fours! Everybody roared with laughter, as Spencer went off a little sheepishly to find Matilda.

The party was a great success, and went on till late at night.

With a mass of stars twinkling above and a big, bright moon coming up over the trees, Timmy said goodbye to the last of his guests.

During the party Matilda and Spencer had set off on their honeymoon, and so, by the time Captain Jones had said goodnight, it was all very peaceful. In fact, that was what Timmy really loved about his new home, it was so quiet and peaceful after all the noise and bustle of False Creek.

To begin with, Timmy missed the excitement and adventure of towing barges and meeting other tugs, but he soon began to make new friends. Captain Jones took him out into Georgia Strait once a week, to keep his engine in good shape and so that he could watch all the tugs and ships going by. Occasionally a tug would be coming through Porlier Pass and the skipper would stop for a chat. One time Timmy was very excited to find that it was Frank, in command of his new tug, with Derek as his mate.

Captain Jones passed the time carving model ships from pieces of driftwood that he found on the beach, and he sold them in the island shops. Matilda and Spencer had their paws full with their first litter of kittens; luckily a kind raccoon had offered to clean and tidy Timmy twice a week, as Matilda was a dreadful housekeeper. In the evenings, Timmy and his old friends spent many happy hours recalling the adventures they had had over the years.

"Shiver me timbers," Captain Jones would say, with a twinkle in his eye, "you've been a working tug for close to seventy years, Timmy. You've really done us proud!"

THE END

THE REAL LIFE TUG ON WHICH TIMMY IS BASED

Steam tug BUSTER B 1938

Kathy K, as she is still named, is one of the oldest **working** tugs on the West Coast

1911 Built for Mr. Buster Brown

1939 Converted to a diesel tug

1964 Renamed **Kathy K**, for the new
       owner's wife Mrs. Kathy Kleaman

1991 Now towing logs up at Bella Colla

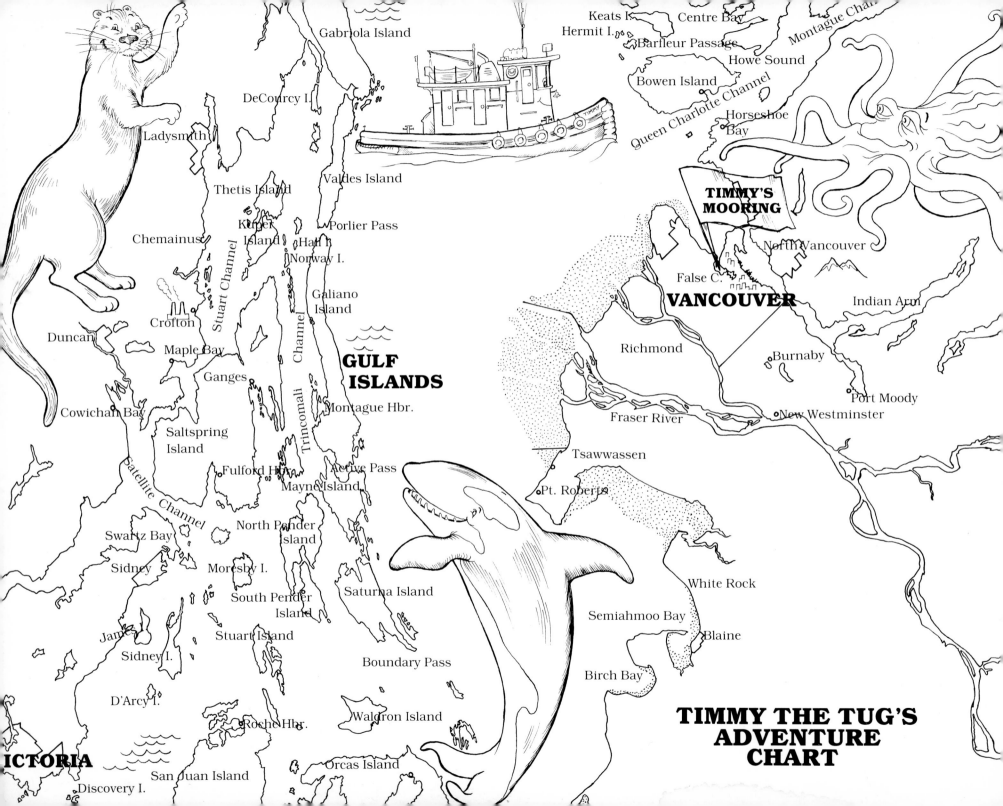

Keats I.
Centre Bay
Hermit I.
Montague Chan.
Barfleur Passage
Howe Sound
Bowen Island
Queen Charlotte Channel
Horseshoe Bay

Gabriola Island

DeCourcy I.

Ladysmith

Valdes Island

Thetis Island
Porlier Pass
Kuper Island
Chemainus
Hall I.
Norway I.

Duncan
Galiano Island

Crofton
Stuart Channel
Trincomali Channel

Maple Bay

GULF ISLANDS

Ganges

Cowichan Bay
Montague Hbr.

Saltspring Island

Satellite Channel
Fulford Hbr.
Active Pass
Mayne Island

Swartz Bay
North Pender Island

Sidney
Moresby I.

South Pender Island
Saturna Island

James I.
Sidney I.
Stuart Island

D'Arcy I.
Boundary Pass

Roche Hbr.

Waldron Island

ICTORIA

Discovery I.
San Juan Island
Orcas Island

TIMMY'S MOORING

North Vancouver

False C.
VANCOUVER
Indian Arm

Richmond
Burnaby

Port Moody

Fraser River
New Westminster

Tsawwassen

Pt. Roberts

White Rock

Semiahmoo Bay
Blaine

Birch Bay

TIMMY THE TUG'S ADVENTURE CHART